How Lazy Can You Get?

by *Phyllis Reynolds Naylor*

ILLUSTRATED BY ALAN DANIEL

A Yearling Book

Published by
Dell Publishing
a division of
Bantam Doubleday Dell Publishing Group, Inc.
666 Fifth Avenue
New York, New York 10103

ISBN: 0-440-40608-0

Reprinted by arrangement with Macmillan Publishing Company on
behalf of the author and Carol Bancroft & Friends on behalf of the
artist.

Printed in the United States of America

April 1992

10 9 8 7 6 5 4 3 2 1

CWO

How Lazy
Can You Get?

To young Robert,
with love

Contents

How Lazy
Can You Get?

ONE

Brasscoat Comes

Mrs. Megglethorp always said that, taken one at a time, each of her children was precious. It was when the three of them put their heads together that something was bound to happen.

"Nonsense, my dear," said Mr. Megglethorp. "It's only because the children are five, nine, and eleven—all of them odd numbers—and when they get to be evens, they'll straighten out, don't you worry."

He had forgotten that when they were four, eight, and ten, they were even more difficult than they were now.

He had forgotten the time they had strung a rope between the top of the garage and the back steps, fastened a bucket to it, and given Goshen, their dog, the ride of his life.

Or the time they had gone into the walnut business and sold nineteen bags before they discovered that some of the nuts were wormy.

And he particularly had forgotten the time his

children had started a newspaper and reported, among other things, which of their neighbors' houses needed painting, and why the Megglethorps had eaten canned tuna three nights in a row.

Timothy, the oldest, was sort of a lay-about, especially in the summer. He loved to lie about on the sofa, or lie about on the rug, or drape himself over the chairs on the porch and think about all the things he did not want to be when he was grown. He did not want to be a vacuum sweeper salesman. He did not want to be a dentist. And he certainly did not want to be someone who wrote advertisements in magazines, because he did not like words that said things they did not mean.

Words such as "New! Improved!" on the same old stuff.

Most of all, he was impatient with grown-ups who did not say what they meant: "In a few minutes, dear," when they meant half an hour, or "Sometime, maybe," when they really meant no.

Amy Megglethorp believed that the best way to be happy was to be left alone. She did not like to be told when to go to bed and when to get up, what to wear and what to eat, or where to play and what she ought to be thinking about.

More than anything else, she did not like being ordered about in the summer after nine whole months of school. If a person found a comfortable place out of the sun, she believed, that person ought to be left alone, whether it was Timothy stretched out on the porch, or Goshen asleep on his back, or Amy herself in the swing with ice cubes between her toes.

Douglas John, the youngest, had long since decided that he did not want to grow up at all. When he was four, however, he had promised himself that always, as long as he lived, he would go on liking to blow bubbles under the bath water and to hang by his knees from the trapeze. Already he had lost interest in bubbles, and this worried him very much.

Grown-ups, he believed, had no imagination whatsoever. His parents could never be persuaded to try the peanut butter toast he fixed for breakfast. They would not let him wear his football helmet to church, even when it was raining, or dig for gold under the back steps or try out his homemade parachute.

The Megglethorp children certainly did not think of themselves as difficult—just common, ordinary types, with missing teeth and scraped elbows. They got along well together unless they were quarreling; they ate all their dinner unless they were full; and they didn't, as a rule, make trouble for anyone except Goshen, who loved every minute of it.

Above all, Timothy, Amy, and Douglas John

were obedient. If Mr. Megglethorp said, "Be quiet," they would see how long they could go without opening their mouths. (Timothy once lasted seven hours and fifty-eight minutes before talking.) If Mrs. Megglethorp said, "Drink your milk, every last drop," Douglas John would turn up his glass and suck and slurp for so long that she would wish she had never said anything at all. And both had learned never to say, "Pick up your rooms before bedtime," because all sorts of things happened when they did.

The parents, of course, loved their offspring very much, no matter how difficult they might be. And when they had to go to Boston for a week one summer on business, they wondered who they could possibly get to stay with the children.

Grandma Megglethorp lived too far away; Aunt Mollie was having a baby; Mrs. Gussman was on vacation; and the Harrigans had moved to Missouri. There was nothing to do but advertise, and that was how Hildegarde Brasscoat called their number.

Miss Brasscoat came highly recommended. She was rated three stars by the National House Managers' Association and was listed in the Guide to Professional Caretakers. It had been some time since she had actually managed a house with *children* in it, but she wore a silver button on her collar for twenty-five years of meritorious service, and that was impressive. She also wore shoes with tractor-tread soles.

Now the Megglethorps were fair-haired and pale-skinned with long narrow faces and pointy chins. They had thin arms and thin legs and, in a strong wind, listed slightly to one side, though they were perfectly healthy, no question about it.

Miss Brasscoat was something else. She was big and round and heavy. She could look at you with one eye while the other was meandering around the room, and when she spoke, her breath came puffing out like steam from an engine. She had a mouth, however, that looked as though it had never smiled. Well, hardly ever, anyway.

The children had been taught to (1) obey their elders; (2) toast their own muffins; and (3) tie a square knot. They had also learned to brush their teeth up and down and wear their socks right side out.

Miss Brasscoat had been taught that (1) children should be seen and not heard; (2) lay-about children were up to no good; and (3) fat children were the very best kind. She especially believed that clean was the only way to come to the table. She never allowed a smudge or a smear under any circumstances.

"If only we could separate the children," Mrs.

Megglethorp told her husband. "I'm sure that Miss Brasscoat would get along fine with any one of them alone, but if they all get an idea at the same time, who knows what might happen?"

"We can't very well lock them in their rooms," said Mr. Megglethorp. "We'll just have to trust them to be on their best behavior."

And so, weighing one thing against another, they decided that Miss Brasscoat and their children should be able to make do from one Friday till the next.

"For goodness sake, be helpful," said Mother as she kissed her brood good-bye. "Answer any questions she might have."

"Try to keep things pleasant," said Father.

And the parents were off to Boston.

TWO

The Trouble Begins

Timothy, Amy, and Douglas John had no intention of bothering Miss Brasscoat. They did not want their parents to worry about them and had already planned some games that Miss Brasscoat might like to play, some records she might like to hear, and some places she might like to go on Sunday afternoon.

But right from the start there were differences. She did not play games, Miss Brasscoat announced as she hung up her clothes in the closet. And she certainly did not care for their kind of music. As for going someplace on a Sunday afternoon, she said, there was plenty to keep them busy right here in the house, what with all the furniture to polish and the floors to scrub and the windows to wash both inside and out.

Something went beep inside Timothy's chest, like a smoke alarm sending off signals. He thought of Hildegarde Brasscoat being in his house for seven days and seven nights, and the something beep-

beeped again, more rapidly. But he was, after all, the oldest, and it was up to him to see that things went smoothly. So he waited till Miss Brasscoat had put on an apron and tidied her hair, and then he showed her about.

It was clear right away that there were other problems as well. Timothy had a hermit crab that lived in a shoebox. Harold was an old crab, a perfectly fine pet. He had a large purple claw, ate dog food, and made absolutely no noise whatsoever. Miss Brasscoat did not like crawly things, however, and became very nervous when Timothy let Harold go scrabbling about on the coffee table.

So the crab was picked back up again and gently carried upstairs to his box.

Amy had a button collection. She enjoyed separating the buttons into those that sparkled and those that didn't, buttons with four holes and buttons with two, buttons that were covered with cloth and those with gold or silver rims. The buttons did not move, had no claws, and never went scrabbling about on the coffee table.

But Miss Brasscoat did not like any buttons that were not hard at work holding things together —unless, of course, it was a button worn on one's collar for twenty-five years of meritorious service. She particularly did not like lay-about buttons that were scattered all over the rug.

So Amy silently gathered up all her buttons and took them upstairs to her room.

As for Douglas John, he had a way of rubbing his left ear when he talked, and this bothered Miss Brasscoat very much. She did not care for such habits, and she did not like ears because she never liked what she found in them. When she saw Douglas John rubbing his, she told him to *stop it at once*.

Douglas John began blinking one eye instead.

Most of all, Miss Brasscoat did not like Goshen. She did not like feet, for one thing, and paws were worse. Tails were not even worth mentioning. And so, when Miss Brasscoat's big rolling eyes came to a stop on the dog, he crept under the sofa and stayed.

It soon turned out that there were some things Hildegarde Brasscoat did like, however. She liked nine o'clock bedtimes and rain boots and Brussels sprouts. She liked piano practice and haircuts and serious conversation at mealtimes. She liked "Yes, Ma'ams," and "No, thank yous," and "Excuse me, pleases." She especially liked thin, pointy-chinned children eating whatever was put on their plates.

At first, having Miss Brasscoat about was a novelty. She knew all sorts of things about all kinds of topics, from insects to earthquakes to Eskimos.

She knew that a horse can see in all directions at the same time, that the elm is the state tree of Nebraska, and that there are twenty-six bones in the human foot. She also wore a whistle around her neck, which drove Goshen absolutely bananas.

The first time she blew it was to announce that dinner was on the table. Never having been whistled for before, the Megglethorp children looked up, shrugged, and went on with their play. Goshen was the only one to amble out to the kitchen, but when he saw Miss Brasscoat with her cheeks all puffed up, blowing the whistle, he dived back under the sofa.

In the mornings Miss Brasscoat went around from room to room in her favorite gray dress, opening doors and blowing her whistle. It was rather like the army, Timothy decided, never having been in the the army, and he bounced out of bed, saluted, and pulled on his jeans.

Amy pretended that it was a fire drill and she had only fifteen seconds to leave a burning building.

But Douglas John didn't take to the whistle at all. He simply pulled the pillow over his head and went back to sleep.

Then there were inspections—ear inspections and fingernail inspections and questions about whose bowels were regular and whose were not. There were

lists of jobs to be done and jobs worth doing over, all stuck to the door of the refrigerator with magnetic clips. There were quizzes about presidents and poets and decimal points and discussions before bed about "What I have learned today that I should have known yesterday."

After a while Timothy decided he did not like the army. Amy was growing very tired of fire drills and quizzes. Douglas John began blinking his eye more and more, and Goshen hid away for hours.

Timothy knew that there was going to be trouble. He could see signs of it all around him. Everytime Hildegarde Brasscoat walked by him, in fact, the beeper in his chest began sending out frantic signals: *Help! May Day! S-O-S!*

After a few days of Miss Brasscoat's attentions, the house had never been more clean or orderly. Chairs gleamed in the kitchen, shoes shone in a row, every book in the living room stood up straight and tall and dusted.

But the Megglethorp children were miserable. Timothy, who liked to lie about all day, was never allowed to lie about at all. Amy, who did not like to be ordered about, was ordered about all the time. Douglas John was more afraid than ever of growing up, and Goshen would go out in the mornings, crawl under the back steps and stay all day.

When Douglas John asked if he couldn't let Goshen sleep in his room, Miss Brasscoat said, "Out!" and her voice was like gravel going down a tin chute.

When Amy questioned the creamed asparagus with broiled tomatoes and mushrooms, Miss Brasscoat said simply, "Eat!" and her voice was like a foghorn at sea.

When Timothy asked if he could please, *please* stay up a half-hour longer to watch *The Revenge of the Termite People,* Miss Brasscoat bellowed, "Bed!" and her deep voice rolled through the house like thunder.

On top of all this, Miss Brasscoat asked the *strangest* questions. When she found Timothy watching a fly crawl about over his hand, she said, "How disgusting can you get?" and whopped the fly with the morning paper.

When she found Amy pulling her Oreo cookies apart and scraping the frosting off with her teeth, she asked, "How revolting can you get?" and whisked the crumbs from the table.

When she found Douglas John blinking his eye, she cried, "How annoying can you get?" and taped his eyelid shut with a Band-aid.

Douglas John began twitching his right shoulder.

How disgusting can you get? How revolting can you get? How annoying can you get? They really should show her, Timothy thought, because something simply had to be done. Amy and Douglas John were very unhappy. Things seemed to be getting worse by the minute.

And every day Miss Brasscoat marked off another square on the calendar.

THREE

Dusting Off
Olde Frothingslosh

It was hot on Tuesday, and the air was heavy.
Fingers stuck together, feet refused to go in shoes,
and Goshen padded about panting, his tongue drip-
ping. It was the kind of day on which Timothy
would have loved to lie about on the porch and
Amy would have loved to spend in the swing and
Douglas John would have enjoyed taking a bath
with Goshen.

Miss Brasscoat, however, decided that it was
a good day for dusting and that each Megglethorp
should do his own room. The beeping feeling in
Timothy's chest began again.

In Douglas John's room, Miss Brasscoat se-
lected the hanging mobiles for special attention, as
well as Lego City and the Ernie puppet with a cigar
in his mouth.

In Amy's room she pointed out the shelf of
glass horses, the clown with ruffles about his neck,

and the row of volleyball trophies. They *were* rather dusty.

In Timothy's room, however, Miss Brasscoat came to a stop so suddenly that the Megglethorps bumped into her from behind. There, against the far wall, was a gigantic pyramid of beer cans— two hundred seventy-eight, to be exact.

It wasn't as though Hildegarde Brasscoat had not noticed the cans before. Timothy had seen her wince the very first time she entered his room. But it wasn't until now that she seemed to see the possibilities of having every one of them dusted, from Olde Frothingslosh on the very top to the ten varieties of Meister Bräu on the bottom.

"I want them dusted," she boomed, her eyes gleaming like the button on her collar.

Timothy gasped.

"What's more," said Miss Brasscoat, bending over the cans and sniffing, "they *smell*. They ought to be washed."

"Washed!" choked Timothy. "They'll rust!"

"Better they should rust than you should rot," said Miss Brasscoat, and told about the brown recluse spider that hides in old, discarded beer cans and other out-of-the-way places. "Wherever it bites you," she said, "gangrene sets in, and a bit of you dies."

After Hildegarde left the room, Timothy, Amy,

and Douglas John sat looking at the two hundred seventy-eight beer cans—the Ballantine they had found in the gutter, the Gunther they had rescued from the trash, the Hapsburg they had paid three dollars for and could have bought for two, and the James Bond 007 for which Timothy had traded twenty of his very best cans.

Even now a brown recluse spider might be laying her eggs inside the red and white Edelweiss, and the newly hatched babies would crawl into the Pabst cans and the Tennent's lager. There would be more eggs and more babies till the whole pyramid had become a giant apartment house for spiders, and when they got tired of living in beer cans, they would creep across the floor to Timothy's bed and down the hall toward Amy's room and on to Douglas John's. . . .

Douglas John was looking at his hands. "If I had nine live fingers and a dead one, could I keep it awhile or would I have to bury it right away?" he asked, his eyes on the cans.

"Right away," said Amy, hugging herself with her arms and glancing cautiously about the room.

"In a coffin?" asked Douglas John.

"No. A matchbox or something," Amy told him. "We'd bury it under the azalea bush." She looked very sad.

Timothy stood up suddenly. "We'll wash out the cans," he said, and it was settled.

They formed an assembly line. Douglas John carried an armload of beer cans into the bathroom, where Amy washed them in the sink. One by one the cans were rinsed, and Douglas John carried them back to Timothy, who dried them off and began to stack them again.

Miss Brasscoat, it seemed, had been right. The sink was soon littered with dirt and stones and pieces of leaves and twigs. An occasional spider egg fell out, and now and then a dead beetle.

It was almost two hours before Olde Frothing-slosh was back in its place of honor at the top of the pyramid. The upstairs had grown hotter and hotter in the heat of the sun, but by three o'clock the other bedrooms were dusted as well, and the children, feeling virtuous, went down to the living room to cool off.

Amy fanned herself with a magazine. Timothy sucked on an ice cube. Douglas John stretched out on the rug with Goshen on his chest.

"It's too hot to play," said Douglas John.

"Too hot to move," said Timothy.

"Too hot to talk, almost," said Amy.

Goshen gave one thump of his tail and let it drop.

For a long time they lay on the rug resting. There was no sound but the clink of ice in Timothy's glass, an occasional thump from Goshen, and the chug of the washing machine below.

Finally they heard Miss Brasscoat's feet on the basement stairs, and a moment later she came through the living room carrying a basket of laundry.

"Honestly, now!" she said. "How *lazy* can you get?" And she stomped on upstairs in her tractor-tread shoes to sort the clothes.

"Let's show her," Timothy said, sitting up.

"Show her what?" asked Amy.

"Just how lazy we can get."

"Why not?" said Amy, and Douglas John began to smile.

So they got some long pieces of string and strung them over a table, a bookcase, and the easy chair, like pulleys. They tied some ends of the strings to the blinds, to both sides of the front door, and to a banana, and the other ends of the strings to themselves.

When Miss Brasscoat came down again, the Megglethorp children were right where she had left them. Timothy, however, was raising and lowering the blinds by lifting one foot. Amy was opening and closing the front door by moving one hand. Douglas John was feeding himself a banana by wagging one

finger. Goshen had rolled over and was playing dead.

Miss Brasscoat stood by the stairs and looked at them. Her eyes never twinkled. Her nose never wrinkled. Her mouth did not widen a bit. Slowly her big chest heaved in and out, and then, without a word, she marched over to the calendar and marked off another day with an X.

FOUR

Rutabaga Jumble

Nobody, Amy Megglethorp decided, could be so long-faced as Miss Brasscoat. It did not seem right to let someone look so unhappy. Being the only daughter in the family, Amy felt she had a special responsibility to see that Miss Brasscoat was welcome in their house. Perhaps if she felt more at home, she would relax a little more and make things easier for all of them.

"She needs a mouth transplant, that's what," complained Timothy the next morning.

"Maybe she could just get herself a whole new head," offered Douglas John. "Even her eyes are grumpy."

But Amy said, "I think that frowning is just a habit with her. If we are especially nice today, maybe she'll be different."

It seemed as though Amy might be right, because when the children came down to breakfast, they found Hildegarde Brasscoat trying her best to be cheerful—as cheerful, that is, as one can get without actually smiling.

"It has come to my attention," she said, over the chipped beef on toast, "that you *did* manage to dust your rooms yesterday as I requested, and that you *did* wash those awful cans. I think that now, perhaps, we shall get along splendidly."

The three Megglethorps smiled pleasantly in return. They wished it would also come to her attention that they did not like chipped beef on toast, but after all, Miss Brasscoat had probably saved their lives. If she had not warned them about the brown recluse, the entire house might have become infested with dangerous spiders. If they owed her nothing more, they were definitely obligated to eat the chipped beef.

Drip . . . drip . . . drop. Something splashed down on the table. *Drip . . . drip . . . drop.*

They all looked up. Water was coming through a small crack in the plaster.

Miss Brasscoat leaped to her feet so suddenly that she overturned the orange juice, which gushed over the side of the table onto Goshen, making him yelp. Timothy, Amy, and Douglas John followed her upstairs and into the bathroom. Someone had left the water dribbling in the sink, the drain was stopped up, and there were puddles everywhere.

Army time again!

"Buckets!" cried Miss Brasscoat.

Amy got the buckets.

"Mop!" ordered Miss Brasscoat.

Timothy got the mop.

"Plunger!" commanded Miss Brasscoat.

Douglas John brought one up from the basement.

Miss Brasscoat tried to unstop the sink, but it was no use, so she finally got a wrench and took the pipe apart. Out fell pieces of leaves and twigs and stones and spiders' eggs, and a couple of dead beetles.

It took all day to put the pipe together again and mop the floor and plaster the ceiling and paint the patch, and Amy felt very guilty. She tried to think what she could do to be helpful. The three pies and two barbequed chickens that her mother had left in the refrigerator were now eaten, and she thought perhaps she could make dinner herself.

"Why don't you rest, Miss Brasscoat?" she suggested. "I can make some hamburgers, and I'll call you when they're ready."

But Miss Brasscoat had other ideas. Thin, pointy-chinned children, she explained, needed all the nutrition they could get, so she was going to cook up something extra special, her very own Rutabaga Jumble, which contained not only ruta-

baga, okra, and eggplant, but every vitamin known to man, and a few more besides.

Now the Megglethorp children had been reared on spaghetti, roast beef, and tossed salad. They knew tomatoes, potatoes, and celery when they saw it, but eggplant, they assumed, had some kind of eggs growing on it; okra sounded like something from the bottom of the ocean; and rutabaga, they were certain, was a disease of the joints. It was not altogether appetizing.

Amy hung around the kitchen to see if she could talk her out of it.

"Have you ever tried chicken pot pie, Miss Brasscoat?" she asked.

"Too starchy," said Hildegarde.

"We could scramble some eggs," Amy hinted.

"Not for dinner," said Miss Brasscoat.

"We aren't terribly hungry," Amy pleaded, but Miss Brasscoat said simply, "You will be when you taste my cooking."

When dinner was ready, Miss Brasscoat blew her whistle, and the children took their seats. There, in the middle of the table, was the Rutabaga Jumble. Miss Brasscoat scooped up a big serving for Timothy. The rutabaga hissed as the spoon went in. Long strands of green okra stretched across the table from the serving dish to Timothy's plate.

"Just a small portion," Amy whispered, but Miss Brasscoat didn't hear and scooped up another large helping. The eggplant oozed onto Amy's plate and rolled over.

Miss Brasscoat dipped up a third scoop for Douglas John. The okra slid off the serving spoon and landed in the butter. By the time it got to his plate, it was more slippery than ever.

Hildegarde Brascoat picked up her fork and began the mealtime quiz which, she declared, aided digestion. Amy would have preferred laughter to aid her own digestion, but she didn't have a choice.

"Who?" asked Miss Brasscoat, "wrote *Hiawatha?*"

Amy did not know that anyone had written him. She thought he was an Indian of long ago who had been born like everybody else. But she made a wild guess.

"Shakespeare?" she asked. Miss Brasscoat winced.

"Socrates?" said Timothy. Miss Brasscoat shuddered.

"Dr. Seuss!" said Douglas John.

Miss Brasscoat pressed her lips together. "Perhaps the Bible would be more appropriate," she said. "Who can tell me why the two bears attacked the children as told in the Book of Kings?"

"There were three bears," said Douglas John, "and they didn't attack anybody."

"Two bears," said Miss Brasscoat firmly. "Don't you remember the prophet Elisha and the story of the two bears?"

Amy tried to remember. She remembered the Ark and the Israelites and the Red Sea and Jonah, but if there was anything in the Bible about bears attacking children, she didn't want to know.

"Because they were bad?" Timothy asked hopefully.

Miss Brasscoat brightened. "Yes, but what exactly did the children do?"

It was time, Amy decided, for some laughter.

"They wouldn't eat their rutabaga," she said.

Timothy and Douglas John howled.

Miss Brasscoat put down her fork. "Don't you children know anything at all?" she asked disgustedly. "How ignorant can you be?"

One of those questions again! The children exchanged glances.

"Amy," Timothy said, rapping on the table, "can you tell me the capital of Arizona?"

"Duh . . ." said Amy, looking ignorant. "Kansas?"

The children shrieked.

"Douglas John," said Timothy, rapping again

for attention. "Who invented the telephone?"

"Duh . . ." said Douglas John. "The Wright brothers?"

The children brayed.

"Timothy," said Amy, taking over, "who discovered the South Pole?"

Timothy went cross-eyed and scratched his head. "Uh . . . duh . . . the penguins!" he shouted.

Douglas John fell off his chair laughing.

"You are excused from this table—*all* of you," said Miss Brasscoat sternly. And with that the Great Stone Face got up and marked off another day on the calendar. Goshen slunk along behind her and snapped at her ankles, but only when her back was turned.

FIVE

The Next to
the Last Straw

Douglas John felt that it was now up to him. Timothy had agreed to wash out his beer cans for Miss Brasscoat, and Amy had offered to cook. All of them had dusted their rooms and picked up their clothes and tried to be pleasant, but nothing had worked. It was time, he decided, to do something about Miss Brasscoat's mouth. It would be a shame if she went through her entire life without smiling even once.

That night, after everyone had gone to bed, the youngest Megglethorp took some strapping tape and crept into her bedroom. There was Miss Brasscoat, propped up against two pillows, sound asleep in the moonlight.

Douglas John stared. She was smiling! Actually smiling! If he could only keep her that way for one entire night, maybe her face would get used to it.

Now his job would be easier. He snipped off several pieces of tape. Carefully, carefully, he stuck a large piece across one side of her mouth, and another criss-crossed on top of that so the smile couldn't sag. Miss Brasscoat snorted and went on smiling.

Douglas John tiptoed around the bed and taped the other side of her mouth. Miss Brasscoat moved her head a little, but went on smiling. He thought of trying to make her eyes crinkle up at the corners while he was at it, but decided to let well enough alone and went back to bed.

The children were awakened Thursday morning by a stomping and snorting in the hallway. Timothy, Amy, and Douglas John rushed from their rooms. There stood Hildegarde Brasscoat in her purple robe, with two big X's made of strapping tape on either side of her mouth. Her mouth was smiling, but her eyes were furious.

"Huh," mumphed Miss Brasscoat, trying to speak, "Huuh duh uh tuh muh?"

She sounded like a frog with lockjaw. Amy quickly helped her unstick the tape.

"Who?" roared Miss Brasscoat, now that her mouth was working again. "Who did this to me?"

"I don't know," said Amy. "I didn't."

"Not me," said Timothy.

They both turned to Douglas John, who was

rubbing one ear, blinking one eye, *and* twitching one shoulder.

"I just wanted to help," he explained uneasily. "I thought . . . if we taped her up for a whole night . . . maybe . . ."

He realized that the tape hadn't helped at all. The corners of Miss Brasscoat's mouth sagged lower than ever, and her voice was seven decibels louder. Her terrible eyes rolled around in her huge head, and for a moment Douglas John thought he would be eaten alive.

It was Goshen's whining that made them all turn around. There he stood, his once-sleek coat stuck to his body in patches. Ten flies were crawling over him, and nine more circled in the air above.

Miss Brasscoat forgot all about the tape and began screaming about Goshen having the mange. But Douglas John remembered the orange juice that she had spilled the day before.

"It's only the orange-juice itch," he said quickly.

"We'll give him a bath, Miss Brasscoat," said Timothy.

So the Megglethorps put on their jeans and shirts and went down to the basement to bathe Goshen while Miss Brasscoat humphed and grumphed and went about making breakfast.

Goshen was so happy to be clean and rid of the

flies that he splashed and yipped and soaked the children thoroughly from head to toe. He jumped up on their jeans and made paw prints on their shirts. When they came upstairs again, wet and wrinkled and covered with dog hair, Miss Brasscoat threw up her hands.

"Timothy, Amy, and Douglas John!" she said, and rushed them outside so that she could mop up their wet footprints. "Just how messy can you get?"

One of those crazy questions again!

Timothy was already leading the way to the garden. Okay, they'd show her. She asked, didn't she?

It had rained during the night, and the garden was muddy. The children walked through it barefoot and felt the mud squish up between their toes. They sat in it, rolled in it, thrust it through their fingers, and gave each other a mud shampoo. Laughing and giggling, they presented themselves once more at the back door—three chocolate-covered children and a dog.

They really hadn't expected her to laugh and she didn't. Hildegarde Brasscoat bellowed like a wild bull and charged. Grabbing them by the collars, she hustled them down the back steps and turned the hose on them. She put their clothes in the laundry, the dog in the basement, and sent them to their

rooms for an hour. This time Timothy realized they had gone much too far.

It was not very pleasant in the Megglethorp house that day. Miss Brasscoat marked it off on her calendar even before lunch, as though she couldn't wait for it to be over. She went about her work silently, her lips pressed together. Even the silver button on her collar seemed dull and disappointed.

By bedtime, the Megglethorps began to wish they could do something to make it up to her. They wished she would talk to them, *scold* them, even. But she sat silently across the room reading *Cannons: The History of the Howitzer,* and finally Timothy, Amy, and Douglas John said good night without response and went upstairs.

Timothy lay awake for a long time. As the oldest, he should have known better. He wondered what his parents would say when Miss Brasscoat told them.

Perhaps, because he was thinking about punishment, he remembered the brown recluse. He wondered if even *before* the beer cans had been washed, a spider might have already crawled out of Olde Frothingslosh and be hiding somewhere in his room.

For a moment he thought of going down to get Goshen, but Goshen would only fall asleep on his bed. Then he remembered Harold, the hermit crab.

Harold wouldn't go to sleep on the job—not if Timothy let him out, he wouldn't. He would be so happy to be free, and so busy exploring the room, that he'd patrol the place all night long. Just let a spider tangle with Harold, and one chomp of his big purple claw would be the end of the brown recluse.

So Timothy got out of bed, took the lid off the shoebox, and helped Harold over the side.

SIX

Harold's Claw

Things were no better the next morning. When the Megglethorps came down to breakfast, they found Miss Brasscoat's bags already packed and waiting by the front door, so that she could leave the minute the children's parents came home.

What's more, Timothy couldn't find Harold anyplace. He looked under his bed, behind his dresser, inside his catcher's mitt, and through all the shoes in his closet. He realized too late that the space under the bedroom door was high enough for Harold to crawl through, and the crab could be anywhere at all in the house.

Timothy did not feel, however, like telling Miss Brasscoat about it. He told Amy, of course, and Douglas John, and they kept their eyes on the floor, especially where Hildegarde's tractor-tread shoes were concerned. But there was no sign of the pet. Even Goshen showed no interest in following the trail when Timothy gave him a sniff of the shoebox. They might never see Harold again.

Despite their worry, the three Megglethorp children tried very hard to be good on this, Miss Brasscoat's last day. They remembered their "Yes, Ma'ams," and "No, thank yous," and "Excuse me, pleases." They did not sit on their napkins or pick their noses or kick each other under the table. They did not even wince when Miss Brasscoat set a serving dish of chipped beef once more in front of them or gag when they noticed the remains of the rutabaga in it.

But Miss Brasscoat, again, was silent. Without so much as "Good morning," or "Pass the butter," or even, "Watch your elbows," Miss Brasscoat picked up the serving spoon.

Suddenly, from up out of the chipped beef rose one big purple claw and waggled about in the air. The spoon fell out of Miss Brasscoat's hand and she shrank back in her chair, clutching her throat.

"Harold!" yelled the Megglethorp children in delight, and Timothy pulled him out.

Miss Brasscoat screamed and turned pale.

"It's only Harold, Miss Brasscoat," Timothy said quickly, and dangled the crab in front of her so she could see it wasn't a lobster or something.

Miss Brasscoat's face turned pink.

"He's not hurt at all," Amy said reassuringly. "He must have been hiding in the serving dish, and you just didn't notice him."

Miss Brasscoat's face turned red.

"We won't tell anyone you tried to bury him alive," Douglas John promised.

Miss Brasscoat's face turned purple.

"Never, never," she shrieked finally, "in all twenty-five years of service have so many things gone wrong in a single week! First the sink stopped up, then water came through the ceiling, then the dog got flies, and now there's a crab in the chipped beef!"

But Harold was not in the chipped beef any longer. He had slipped out of Timothy's hands and was trying to maneuver around the table. There was cream sauce on one set of legs and okra on the other.

"Get him off the table this instant!" said Miss Brasscoat, poking at him with a spoon and trying desperately to look as though she were in control of herself once more.

Harold, however, was not in control of anything, least of all his eight legs. As the children at-

tempted to head him off, he slithered around the butter, tumbled off the edge of a saucer, and bumped into the sugar bowl.

"Oh, for goodness sake!" Miss Brasscoat frowned, but there was the teeniest, tiniest catch in her voice.

It could have been a small hiccup. It could have been a mere cough. But to the Megglethorp children, it sounded suspiciously as if it might possibly, by the barest chance, be laughter.

At that moment, poor Harold skidded on a piece of rutabaga and went sailing down the table as though it were a ski slope, his legs flying. Around Amy's orange juice he went, between the salt and pepper shakers, and finally crash-dived upside down on the toast.

Miss Brasscoat started to wheeze, and her big gray eyes crinkled at the corners. The wheeze became a chuckle, and slowly, like old leather beginning to crack, her face began to smile. Then the miracle happened; Hildegarde Brasscoat laughed.

It was a great, magnificent, deep-chested, lung-stretching sound—like a laugh that had been trapped in Miss Brasscoat for twenty-five years and was just bursting to get out. Her cheeks shook and her eyes watered, and she threw back her head and let it come.

"M . . . Merciful heavens!" she gasped. "I don't know what is the matter with me! How silly can I get?"

One of those questions again!

Timothy, Amy, and Douglas John gathered around her.

"Show us, Miss Brasscoat!" Amy begged. "How silly *can* you get?"

"Good gracious, how ridiculous!' bellowed Miss Brasscoat, holding her sides.

"Go ahead, Miss Brasscoat, show us!" said Timothy.

"What nonsense!" she said, wiping her eyes.

"Please!" cried Douglas John. "What is the silliest thing you can think of?"

Hildegarde Brasscoat folded her arms over her stomach and thought about it. "Well," she said, "the silliest thing I can think of is a parrot I once saw down in Sarasota, Florida."

"A parrot?" asked Timothy.

"Yes, indeed, a parrot. It sat on a perch outside a barber shop. All day long it stepped back and forth, from one claw to another. Like this. . . ."

Miss Brasscoat climbed up on a kitchen chair. She tucked her hands under her arms like wings. First she lifted up one leg straight out at the side. "Aawk, aawk," she said. Then the other leg. "Aawk. Aawk."

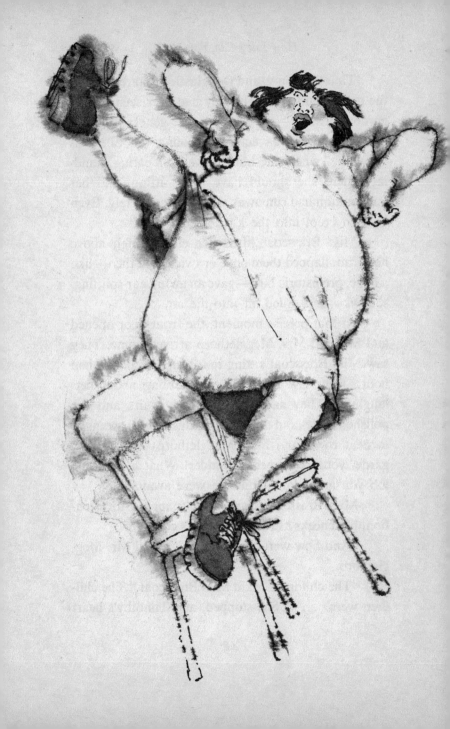

Timothy, Amy, and Douglas John stared. It was the most wonderful sight they had ever seen. Hildegarde Brasscoat—the sergeant, the general, the human bassoon—was actually goofing off. She was "aawking" when she should have been eating, standing where she should have been sitting, and her imagination had run away with her completely. Even Goshen crept into the kitchen to watch.

Miss Brasscoat lifted her elbows high above her head, flapped them once or twice, and then—like a huge, prehistoric bird—gave an awful, ear-splitting, squawk—and sailed off into the air.

At that precise moment, the front door opened and Mr. and Mrs. Megglethorp arrived home. They saw Miss Brasscoat sitting in a heap on the kitchen floor. They saw the children tumbling about her, laughing. They saw the gleaming chairs and the polished tables and the books all dusted and arranged in neat rows, and Mrs. Megglethorp said, "Hildegarde, you are indeed a wonder! What a fine, fine job you have done while we were away."

Miss Brasscoat leaped up, snapping to attention, her cheeks as red as Goshen's collar.

"And how were the children?" asked Mr. Megglethorp.

"The children?" said Miss Brasscoat. "The children were. . . ." She stopped, and Timothy's heart began its beepity-beeping again. *I won't tell if you won't,* her eyes seemed to say. "Well, I just might miss them very much," she answered.

Mr. Megglethorp told her that the cab was waiting, and the children lined up to say good-bye. Timothy and Douglas John shook her hand, Amy patted her cheek, and Goshen crept over and licked her cautiously on the ankle. She got in the cab with her bags, her button, her whistle, her shoes with the tractor-tread soles, and—her smile.

As for the brown recluse spider—Amy thought she was dying the next morning when she woke up to find that one of her fingers had turned green.

"It's only paint off the toy we brought you," said her father.

"I thought it was gangrene,' said Amy.

"Why would you think that?"

"I thought I'd been bitten by a brown recluse spider," Amy told him.

"There aren't many brown recluse spiders around here," said her father.

"Not even in old beer cans?" asked Timothy.

"No. Not in this part of the country."

Miss Brasscoat didn't know everything.

Timothy thought about it. If he hadn't been scared of spiders, he wouldn't have let Harold out of the shoebox. If Harold hadn't slipped out of his room, he wouldn't have crawled in the serving dish. If it wasn't for Harold and the chipped beef, Miss Brasscoat would never have laughed. And that was the most marvelous thing that had happened in a long time, because it meant that people, even grown-ups, could change.

They didn't discover until later that Miss Brasscoat seemed to have taken Douglas John's ear-rubbing, eye-blinking, and shoulder-twitching with her, because slowly those habits just disappeared. And she had either forgotten to cross off the last day on the calendar or decided that somehow, maybe, she didn't quite want it to end after all.

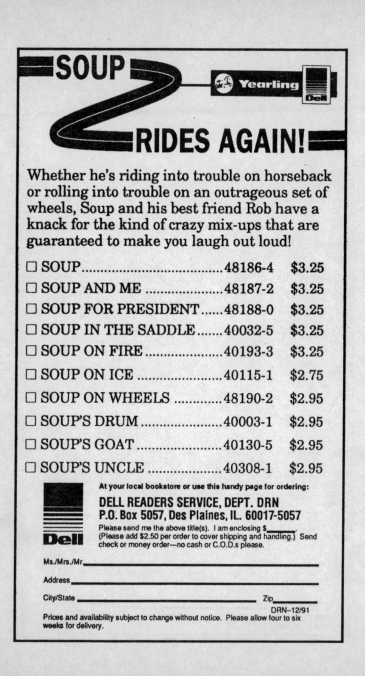

SOUP

Yearling Dell

RIDES AGAIN!

Whether he's riding into trouble on horseback or rolling into trouble on an outrageous set of wheels, Soup and his best friend Rob have a knack for the kind of crazy mix-ups that are guaranteed to make you laugh out loud!

☐ SOUP 48186-4 $3.25

☐ SOUP AND ME 48187-2 $3.25

☐ SOUP FOR PRESIDENT 48188-0 $3.25

☐ SOUP IN THE SADDLE 40032-5 $3.25

☐ SOUP ON FIRE 40193-3 $3.25

☐ SOUP ON ICE 40115-1 $2.75

☐ SOUP ON WHEELS 48190-2 $2.95

☐ SOUP'S DRUM 40003-1 $2.95

☐ SOUP'S GOAT 40130-5 $2.95

☐ SOUP'S UNCLE 40308-1 $2.95

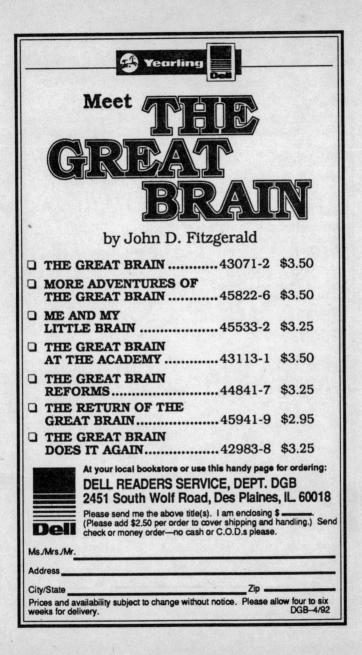